THE MONSTER, THE MERMAID, AND DOCTOR MENGELE

THE MONSTER, THE MERMAID, AND DOCTOR MENGELE

Ian Watson

NewCon Press
England

First published in the UK February 2021 by
NewCon Press
41 Wheatsheaf Road,
Alconbury Weston,
Cambs, PE28 4LF

NCP251 (limited edition hardback)
NCP252 (paperback)

10 9 8 7 6 5 4 3 2 1

ISBN:

978-1-912950-76-8 (hardback)
978-1-912950-77-5 (paperback)

Cover art and front cover design by Mabel SustanciaGris
Back cover layout by Ian Whates

Typesetting and editorial meddling by Ian Whates
Text layout by Ian Whates

One

Here we are in the 1960s, perhaps. Up the wide river Paraná pushing against the current comes a small personal steamer carrying the elusive war criminal Doctor Josef Mengele, 'Angel of Death', on its upper deck. They seek him here, they seek him there. But he also is seeking – from a canvas chair below a canopy Mengele directs his Carl Zeiss binoculars befitting a U-boat commander towards the westerly bank of the river, tangled and semi-tropical.

A German Shepherd bitch sprawls nearby, grand-pup of a former guard dog saved from Auschwitz-Birkenau as the Red Army drew ever closer to the concentration camp.

As well as being Doctor before the Nazi regime and the SS expired, Mengele was also Hauptsturmführer, a senior assault leader. 'Captain', in less bombastic lingo.

Ranks and qualifications are important. Discomforting news reaches Mengele's ears that to comply with this new era the University of München may strip away Josef's doctorate in anthropology. Furthermore, the University of Frankfurt may cancel Mengele's medical PhD *cum laude* awarded for cleft palate and cleft chin research. An intolerable prospect. The yiddishe Hollywood star Kirk Douglas makes a fortune from his cleft chin.

Mengele lights the fifteenth or twentieth Palermo of the hot moist morning. The tin ashtray of butts is filling up fast. Momentarily rage fills Josef that his doctorates might be set aside. Such red-hot rage usually only lasts ten seconds or so.

In the circumstances, how timely came the eye-witness account yesterday by that tribesperson. A pureblood native. In itself this is laughable, comparable with Aryan purity, yet it's still a distinct cut above the Mestizo mongrelry of most Paraguayans. The trouble with Paraguay racially is that plenty of ambitious Spanish males came to the interior but not nearly enough adventurous Spanish ladies. Thus a law ordained that lusty Iberian bachelors must find native brides with whom to breed. The absurdity! As if genuine Germans heeding the *Drang nach Osten* impulse to head eastwards should then spill their seed amongst Slavs of slanty eyes betraying the original mongolism of many Slavs. That trueblood Tupí informant's eyes were just a bit slanty – true to Indian form, as was the tribesman's broad nose.

Mengele employs walleyed mix-race Tomás as a handyman Jack-Of-All who can interpret forms of Guaraní including Mixture into Spanish which Mengele can mostly follow.

Here is a *report* by an *eye-witness* now physically present, not a mythic yarn from years gone by. The shortish native's shoulders are strapping. Swarthily tanned, jet-black hair. Mengele gazes into the eyes of the teller and sees truth there. A tale of a *mermaid* on a lonely stretch of the vast river, *'una sirena auténtica, señor'* – *Eine echte Nixe*, Josef translates to himself – not some vagrant Amazonian manatee. A substantial mermaid with a beauteous bosom, hair of coppery gold, and a tail of silver scales.

Natives up and down the river are aware that 'the Doctor' will pay a bunch of good green *guaraníes* for news of conjoined twins and other freaks of childbirth. Research must continue. Israeli agents hunting for the Doctor haven't the foggiest and search in all the wrong places in the wrong countries using the wrong photos. The CIA thinks Mengele is a car mechanic.

Even as the informant watched from his *canoa* masked by dangling fronds, of a sudden a submerged anaconda arose and seized the mermaid around her midriff smoothly bereft of any navel. A mighty muscular green anaconda of the boa family, largest snake in the world and secondmost in length! This anaconda probably isn't a Yellow but a female Green visiting all the way from Amazonia.

(This telling occurred at Mengele's fortress-hacienda the day before Josef boards his wood-burning steamer *Flosshilde*, she being the name of one of Wagner's Rhinemaidens.)

The great boa begins to manoeuvre the mermaid as she thrashes her tail and utters a siren shriek. Oh yes, the serpent has a crush on her and wants to drown her.

Yet someone or something has far more than just a crush upon the mermaid. Verily, a fanatical devotion! For out of foliage leaps a valiant Tarzan! To be helpful, the Tupí chap mimics a cinema screen and ululates – yet *this* lord of the jungle is something else than he whom Edgar Rice Burroughs portrayed.

"This grotesco Tarzan is a mighty monster man," interprets Tomás. "Taller than I can push my hand high enough. Around his loins he wears skin of a jaguarete –"

Since this tribesperson himself is 'swarthy' – is that the appropriate word? – may we also please mention that Mengele himself looks a bit *gypsy*? Touch of the tarbrush. Not so different from folks such as Josef sent by the thousands to be gassed and furnaced. Rather than Josef being blond and Nordic. Maybe that's why to compensate Mengele wore his Captain's cap so jauntily cocked to one side while he selected arrivals at the railway ramp in Auschwitz, nonchalantly whistling opera airs through the gap between his top two front teeth. And the bush-hat he sports on the steamer – never without a hat, him – is askew to distract attention from his big betraying brainy forehead which even plastic surgery fails to minimise.

In truth the skin of Mengele the Merciless is tawny and his hair is dark brown, while his eyes are a piercing greeny-brown. His walrus moustache is very Nietzsche, although there's also an ethnic look as in the Gaucho cowboy style which is traditional for a long way around here. Josef blends in.

"– Both the Tarzan's legs seem be like part-bull and part-horse. His chest is sewn leather from the Pampas, yeah patchwork. His head is square-square-square." Like a cube? "Like nothing me never saw. Big, wide, high him. Down leaps this Gigant woooomph upon that boa in the water. BANGSPLAT down comes his scaly pineapple-fist upon the serpiente as upon overripe watermelons. Boa she jerks upward, bringing into vista a lot of massive anaconda. Then boa she submerges, to make escape – also to drown the Mermaid. Does that Gigant fear his beloved may drown? *Can* a mermaid drown?"

Dr Mengele PhD PhD is wondering similar things, swiftly imagining photographs and dissections and preservation of specimens and bottling in formaldehyde, then the subsequent writing-up and despatching to Deutschland where the universities will scarcely dare to undoctor him after he reveals to science an authentic *Homo sirena*. Or should that be *Homo nympha*? His conduct at Auschwitz surely must be condoned. Obviously during wartime anaesthetic shall be reserved for warriors. Is it to Josef's *advantage* that restrained patients squirm and scream, eh now, is it? Remember that afternoon when those gypsy twins were grafted back to back...? Perhaps we would rather not know about this!

And that monstrous superman with the power of a bull multiplied by a horse... from where exactly had that one come? From the imaginary island of Dr Moreau, eh?

Or from a possible rival of Josef Mengele himself?

Who might that rival be? Maybe SS Hauptsturmführer Aribert Heim, Butcher of Mauthausen? Or some other decamping Death Doctor? In the vast rainforests and jungles of South America are many private places where a well-protected scientist can continue his career under cover.

"– The Tarzan seizes and squeezes that anaconda of boa family snake. Yeah he puts the squeeze on the squeezer just as the Mermaid runs out of shriek, beneath an overhanging coral tree in full bloom that may make later for her a scarlet wreath afloat upon the waters vast as a sea –"

The sheer specificity of the account! The Ceibo tree, *Erythrina crista-galli*...

Patron tree of two nations! This has to be a true eyewitness report! *Ein echt Augenzeugenbericht!*

"The Tarzan is not demented in his behaviour," hears Josef impressionistically in Spanish. "Why is the boa so fat? Because she has babies inside her. Fifty or sixty baby boas seventy centímetros long by now have hatched from the erstwhile big orange eggs within.

Many metres back in my canoa I catch a whiff of protective stench from her now open cloaca. During all the gestificating of snakelets inside their eggs Mama Boa she has not eaten a bite. She is starving, which is why she gripped tight the Mermaid to drown the Sirena for convenient slow swallowing soon after the babe-boas are born. But now Tarzan he squeezes Mama Boa so that eel-long babes burst from her stinky cloaca right away into the water a bit before those babes are *quite* prepared to flee and to hide. They've been packed tight and slithery inside her, a barrel of baby boas. Instinct is all very well but the babies' lack of river practice brings a shoal of hungry red-bellied pirañas for a feast-frenzy. Mama Boa she is driven to distraction! Would you want frenzied pirañas biting your cloaca bloody paying no heed to the foulness of its stench? What a bubbling of sangre and ichors there is in the waters! Mama Boa she turns over, casting off Sireñorita Mermaid, whom Señor Tarzan he snatch up in his mighty Johnny Weissmuller arms, raising the Sireñorita up to breathe, her bounteous bosoms filling. Then Tarzan he rush back into the jungla carrying La Mermaid and that is all I see. Though I think to me –"

Mengele addresses the native informant directly: "Jawohl, Sí, Yes, what did you think to you?" Which Tomás translates.

"I think that a Mermaid may have a copulatory cloaca amid her silver scales the way an anacardo oops I mean *anaconda* boa has a cloaca."

Indeed this may explain much about the relationship of Tarzan and the Mermaid. This tribesperson fully deserves his tip-off pay.

Mengele reclines vigilantly aboard *Flosshilde*. Not a rustbucket by any means, albeit a bit past her best. The vessel is crewed by a trio of mixed-blood Mestizos comprising Tomás, Alfonso the cook, and helmsman Enrique.

In the *Ring of the Nibelungs* the *Tarnhelm* is a magical helmet which can cause invisibility. At times hot mists veil their vessel. Maybe Mengele ought to have named his steamer *Tarnhelm* but no, he doesn't need any screening from benighted bumbling searchers, and mists won't help him to spot a mermaid.

Across the awning whereunder Mengele keeps watch, an improvised rocket net lies folded like some giant nylon accordion ready to streak forth across the waters for up to fifty metres. Any Hemingway-type sportsman hunting hereabouts for fierce giant Golden Dorados with pitbull jaws will use a large seductive fly on a line. A mermaid, though, isn't likely to snap her jaws at a fly however orchid-like and costume-jewelish that fly is, even if mermaids are notoriously narcissistic, forever admiring themselves in medieval mirrors. Supposing that blooms are to the Sireñorita's taste, her Tarzan can pick umpteen jungle flowers for her. There shall be no list here of available blooms! We aren't obsessively Humboldt with his passion for environment, later renamed ecology as we slide closer to planetary extinction. Due to all the fish in the river a line cannot be baited with Brazilian bonbons, which would soon melt anyway. Let's face it, this mermaid cannot be snared by the mouth. Unless with honeyed words perhaps. No: there must be a net.

The metal pipes charged with black powder plus electric blasting line and other kit have previously been given a successful test; consequently, dear reader, the spectacle *will not happen* of the awning being torn off from *Flosshilde* nor of the boat being pulled over upon its side and sinking. When the twin rockets blast off sidewards, just expect some pitch and slosh. Tomás the Jack-Of-All is in charge of the rocket net.

Even so, *luring* the Mermaid to the hullside of the steamer is preferable because then the weighted net can simply fall down upon her without any noisy fireworks. And she may indeed swim up close to the boat's hull, for isn't it said that Mermaids love to lure lusty males to their doom by drowning them? Achtung, Idiot und Trottel! This Sireñorita cannot be just any old mythic mermaid! She has to be a product of dedicated supremely skilful specialist surgery. Of SS-SS, performed by a rival PhD.

After the mighty Amazon, this river is the second longest of South America. Three thousand miles in length plus loose change. As of now in the 1960s, few dams interrupt its main flow or its many tributaries. The era of escalating energy greed and global warming is still a gasping tadpole ahead. In the Sixties Homosaps are only starting to dam for hydro power all rivers within reach upon the planet, each river multiple times like junkies jolting their veins.

Returning to the same stretch of riverbank identified by the tribesperson doesn't guarantee another glimpse, let alone a netting, of La Sireñorita nor a tranquillisation by dart-gun of Big Boyfriend. Should there some day be a dam, does Tarzan the Mermaiden's boyfriend detour through the jungle, herself lasciviously slippery in his arms, otherwise slung over his mighty shoulders in a fireman's lift? At other times does Tarzan ride upon his ladyfishbride while the Sireñorita swims powerfully along the Paraná? This is idle fantasising. Only practical science and experiment will reveal the truth.

By the century upcoming the Tarzan will or would have his work cut out carrying the Mermaid in his arms around dozens more such obstacles through any surviving jungle, or private gardens, or parking lots. Gott, how *old* may the Tarzan and his Mermaid bride be already?

Mengele is following his star, that same star which magically leads his persecutors far astray. If Mengele the Merciless concentrates hard enough upon this riverbank, surely he will succeed. Though will the Mermaid and her Monster-Man survive their encounter with Herr Doktor Mengele?

However, that man-und-Übermensch aboard the steamer is the *Mythic Mengele*, not the Mundane Mengele. On board *Flosshilde* is a master escape-artist of superhuman skill who time and again has easily dodged agents of Mossad, and of the Federal German Government, and of the CIA and the FBI and Interpol, and of the world's press corps panting in pursuit, as well as top Nazi-hunter Simon Wiesenthal. 1977 will be the year of Wiesenthal's lurid widescreen lie in *Time* magazine about Mengele living in armed luxury in Asunción, so as to prime the pump of paying for more pursuit. They seek him here, they seek him there. And how the hunters exaggerate and what outright lies they tell! Reliant on publicity which leads to funding in an impeccable cause, as well as to journalistic jaunts, collectively all of these hunters conspire via hysterical headlines and hushed-up blunders to create the masterful Mengele protected on his secret jungle ranch by savage German Shepherds or Doberman Pinschers, a Mengele who – should he need to – can quickly dive for safety to some Nazi bolthole in distant Lima Peru beside the Pacific Ocean very far from the Paraná, just for instance. *This* supremely capable Mengele breeds Boys from Brazil. He is Marathon Man Mengele, rich with diamonds robbed from murdered Jews. This is Mato Grosso Mengele surrounded by Indian bodyguards armed with Mauser carbines and curare blowpipes. He has Nazi gold.

By the way, in this narrative we are somewhat conflating big Argentina, vast Brazil, and tucked-away Paraguay across a range of years. Those who sought Mengele blundered similarly! There was even a time when the Israeli intelligence operative in charge of the

15

Nazi escape desk couldn't understand any German or Spanish, only English and Hebrew: fat lot of use.

Mundane Mengele patrols a potato farm accompanied by an entourage of a dozen or so yapping stray mongrels so skinny they appear to be assembled from matchsticks. But dear me, the phrase 'Mengele's Mangy Mutts' lacks the frightening frisson of 'The Doktor's Deadly Dobermans'.

Whatever the breed may be, Mengele the Mutilator's mythic dawgs bound through the Paraguayan jungle along almost imperceptible native dirt paths. Except that they don't. The Captain who once selected people for extermination or experiment nowadays grades potatoes. As for access to an El Dorado of Nazi gold, dream on.

Mengele's family back in (for the sake of anonymity) 'Goonzburg' Bavaria secretly support their absconded mass-murdering war criminal as best they can, making him the agent in Paraguay for their lucrative Mengele manure spreader, the best postwar scatterer of beast-shit in Europe. When in Josef's opinion Paraguay gets too hot for safety, he buys a shabby flat in São Paulo. A housemaid/cook sleeps in a garden shed, and he's lovesick for her like a lost puppy.

Mundane Mengele acquires slipped discs, prostate problems, high blood pressure, nerves, migraines, and allergies, as well as an aching inner ear, rheumatism, depression, a leg swollen by some insect bite. As a doc he understands his complaints and makes sure to complain given any opportunity. Even so, he's still swimworthy in the sea, off one of São Paulo's fine beaches.

He drinks litres of milk and sleeps with a Mauser under his pillow. Probably the compact self-cocking-hammer model. Nice wooden grip.

This is the banally dotty and anal Mengele who writes forty pages of autobiography upon the subject of his own birth including a page and a half devoted to his placenta. On a higher note of self-pity, Josef reads Ovid's *Elegies* and the Roman poet's letters from exile by the Black Sea.

As *Flosshilde* steams onward, Mythic Mengele softly sings the words following the Prelude to *Das Rheingold*. Shall we say *Das Paranágold*? The prize which will protect his PhDs. Which will maybe elevate him *in absentia* to a Professorship? Is this 'megalomania'? Maybe mengelemania?

What jerks the strings of the mundane Mengele isn't megalomania but paranoia (no connexion with paraná nor piranha) – although, did our Josef but know it, he's enjoying the luck of the very Devil – and his luck will last right up until the end. *Almost* to the last few moments. Absolute ends are rarely lucky.

Mythic Mengele sings softly, undulatingly, phonetically to the plashing of the mighty Paraná:

"Veia! Vaga! Voge, du Velle,
    valle zur Viege! und so weiter –"
which one might express as:

"Wickedly wily! Watery! Wavy!
Weepy and washy! whirlpooly! –"

As the day wears on, Captain-Doktor Josef proceeds to hum Siegfried's triumphalist *Rhine Journey* which doesn't have any words. Then Josef eats a grilled fillet of Dorado, reeled in battlingly to be gutted and prepared by Alfonso who has quite a gut himself. Even while eating the flaky white fatty fish-flesh Mengele watches steadfastly through the Zeiss glasses.

Dorado is a powerful and vicious fish, big as a pit-bull and with similar jaws. By keeping away from the river banks, the Mermaid can avoid snappy redbelly piranhas, yet what of cruising carnivores such as Dorados? To deter predators, does the Sireñorita's cloaca – suppose she possesses such a piece of anatomy! – stink abominably yet unnoticeably by her Tarzan... who may be *anosmic*, lacking any sense of smell? The Doktor may have some delicate dissecting to do, while curare paralyses his patient – without in the least diminishing the intensity of pain. Agony is regrettable since the ideal would be that the patient could be questioned during dissection, his or her mouth and vocal chords remaining under voluntary control, though not to scream, simply to speak. And to be able to answer questions during later stages of dissection and vivisection.

Reliable Tomás and Enrique and/or Alfonso will take turns to keep the paralysed patient alive by pumping the bellows to deliver air through a tracheostomy, a hole in the windpipe. Way back in 1825 such was the first method of maintaining life, pioneered experimentally upon a female donkey paralysed by curare. Out in the back of beyond a bellows proves beneficial. You can operate quietly without the dual racket of generator and air-pump. In the case of a test subject incapacitated by a shot of curare but needing chasing down, a scalpel to cut the windpipe plus the bellows to insert as pump is the perfect lightweight mobile first aid kit.

Months earlier, Mengele commanded Alfonso to order by way of smugglers a curare antidote, a cure-curare as it were. Smuggler-criminals would have better security and secrecy where an unusual pharma item is involved. Since the Nineteenth Century the University of Vienna had specialised in identifying the complex formulas of chemicals extracted from plants. Very valuable chemicals in many cases, such as physostigmine derived from the calabar bean – being no less than an acetylcholinesterase antagonist antidote to curare poisoning. How Nature provides!

Anyway, a selective local-antianaesthetic contra-curare drug has now become available, whereby reportedly whispery speech – or whispery screaming – is possible for a paralysed patient. May this drug arrive at Josef's door during his current absence!

Two

Hot jungly Paraguay, wide and flat, is home to a multitude of diseases and misfortunes spread by parasites and pests. Hookworm and hepatitis and dysentery and typhoid and malaria and TB, to name but six. The crew of the *Flosshilde* may have their fair share of several. Plus, there's a bonus splurge of Chagas disease across the superhot dry Chaco Region causing swelling hearts and bloated colons. Where better than that wild west Chaco to hold a long war? Chagas is named after an actual chap. Although he did not wear cowboy chaps.

However, it's Josef's own ever-wretched condition about which he grouses semi-comprehensibly to his crew during the lazy afternoon as a way of staying awake while he keeps watch, alternately rambling then ranting for a minute maximum. Rheumatism! Migraines! Raging blood pressure! His swollen pee-squeezing prostate! Allergies to most everything except for milk! The galley's kerosene-powered fridge buzzes away faintly from the galley below, keeping Josef's milk supply unsour.

That evening comes a terrible storm...

The thunder is deafening Donner und Blitzkrieg so titanic that it could drown out the noise of a naval battle. Fork lightning is molten silver and darting mercury, vertical rivers and tributaries and deltas of uncontrollable energy. Sheet lightning becomes a bombardment of lividly blue, violet, and purple bruises across a wide warfront cum waterfront. Wild winds whip and rip. Rain lashes and smashes. As Enrique struggles to lodge *Flosshilde* into one of the creeks denting the bushy bank, there comes another blinding flash like the Norse rune for victory...

... and all of the gunpowder destined for the rocket-net detonates, goading *Flosshilde*'s boiler to explode too... OOOOMPH-WHOOOOMPH.

Not *lethally* as regards Mengele. Propellingly, though! Concussively, though. Disruptingly and displacingly so! (Of the crew's fate, and the dog's, we know as yet nada.)

Mengele stirs. Apparently he's inside a raggedy hut of palm branches tangled with mossy boughs lopped long ago. Vaguely he remembers dragging himself from soaking darkness where walls of water marched into merely drippy darkness like some crippled beast encountering a cave of sorts wherein to hide. Outside, the forest murmurs to itself from the first act of *Siegfried* until parrots start to screech. Dilute sunlight shafts greenly through burgeoning foliage glimpsed between gaps in the wall of palm fronds. Genocidal ecocidal mercenaries of capitalism have not yet swarmed hereabouts.

In one direction the tiny hut is darker. Ah, a wall of fronds separates the primitive side-shed of Josef's salvation from what must be a bigger dilapidated native hovel.

As the raucous neighbouring wildlife quits its morning cacophony for a while, Mengele crawls towards human words, low voices becoming audible... and sounding like German speech!

Touch of a Munich accent there? Tad further north? Ingolstadt, town of the university? Certainly somewhere within Josef's own beloved Bavaria! *How can this possibly be?*

"You will recall, Liebchen –" whereupon Josef cops a partial glimpse of no less than the mightily muscled and thewed *Tarzan* of his informant's description!

As though narrating is a regular routine of affectionate bonding between the Monster-Man and the Mermaid – here's an accompanying flash of silver scales, would a scalpel break upon those? – the Tarzan proceeds to recount amazing things.

"You will recall, my Darling, how I first came to fully functional existence and ego, being gifted with conscious life when lightning energised my brain and my brawn by way of the Franklin kite conductor which Victor Franklinstein flew during a storm as fierce as yestern storm..."

What, Franklin the *Amerikanisch Elektriker*, and *Politiker?* Dr Mengele himself certainly carried out electrical experiments upon strapped-down girl patients to test their resistance to pain. About fifty per cent died.

The mermaid's voice is lullingly liquid, her tone teasing and tinkly. As well as liquid it's staccato like discreet acoustic bubbles. This might have to do with the pattern of her breathing.

"Nay my love.but as usual.you mean Victor Frankenstein."

"Nay," with a big chuckle, "but I was not even able to speak articulately to start with – you may expect some confusion."

And did Josef just hear Victor *Frankenstein?*

For just a few moments let us regard Victor Frankenstein as the most dedicated of death doctors, sewing together parts of dead people aiming to reanimate them! Nay, not only did Frankenstein stitch together bits of *people* but also parts of big beasts. Some bits of humans were too fiddly to finger about with. Herr Doktor Frankenstein relied for organs and limbs not merely upon dissection rooms and graveyards but also upon *slaughterhouses* – the transient tenants of which were not human corpses but sheep and bulls and pigs.

Yet... surely Victor Frankenstein is... fictive?

Mengele is cultivated and well-read. Exiled forever from Bavaria, he reads Ovid's epistles from exile despatched to Rome from amongst the rough nomads by the Black Sea. Mengele appreciates Goethe and Rilke and Novalis. Such authors make it worthwhile being a German!

Is Frankenstein really a *Figur* from fiction? Reality and illusion swim in confluence for Josef.

"After my cruel rejection by my maker I learned Deutsch like a parrot while lurking for survival in Ingolstadt as well as outside where wood-cutters dwelled. Much later I found myself in a hut adjoining the home of a blind old man and his impoverished family where I learned some gentle Französich."

"So you did.my darling."

"Ach yet the francophone family found me out, Liebling, distorted giant that I am."

"Whose member so pleasures my vent!"

"All too soon I knew the hatred towards a Monstro that is almost instinctive among so-called 'humanity'. For my clumsy creator made me the denizen of an uncanny valley – *ein unheimliches Tal.* I who sought humans to touch was inhumanely rebuffed."

"Yet you only murdered.very selectively .compassionately.with paltry pain. Moment of surprise. flame of life snuffed.very next second.Too speedy for terror on the part of target.Good like a guillotine. without any run-up. You killed only to bargain.so I may be created.for you to adore!"

Does she have a name? How can she have a name, unless it's a name given to her by the Monster? Yet how can a Nameless One name somebody else?

Now let's see... the oft iterated utterance of You, namely *Du Du Du Du* (quite a Bavarian noise)... might result in the name Dudu! *Sie Sie Sie Sie* (courteous address) might result in the name Zizzi. Consequently: Dudu and Zizzi, Monster and Mermaid.

"Dearest Zizzi," continues Dudu indeed – for Josef is intuitive if not blessed with much empathy – "I brought about the deaths of selected targets until Victor Frankenstein vowed to manufacture me a helpmate – upon receipt of whom we both, She and I, would hasten to South America here to hide ourselves happily forevermore within the vast jungles of this continent... although nowadays these blessèd jungles, these harmonious Humboldtian forests, these selvas themselves are plunged in peril and shaved and gutted due to Man and to Kapitalism."

This Man-Made Monster has heard of *Kapitalism*? As well as of Alexander von Humboldt?

"When you say Helpmate.dear Dudu," responds Zizzy, "I perforce add.'without issue'.to the word 'mate'."

"Will you forever regret, Beloved Zizzi, our incapacity to conceive?"

This whole exchange is riveting to Mengele, not least due to Josef working as an abortionist for women in Argentina, also as a vet artificially inseminating cows in Paraguay. Conceivably Dudu might be the one who is *riveted* in the tissue-stapling sense of the word? Ach no, back in the early Nineteenth Century Frankie would obviously *sew* stitches – seamster surgery, tissue tailoring that was. Back, indeed, *to repeat*, in the early Nineteenth Century! By now Dudu must be 143 years old (and his Bride 142 or so). Both the Monster and the Mermaid Bride rejoice in longevity. Or maybe they bemoan their fate? – if Josef's own body is anything to go by!

Back in the day, Ingolstadt University was full of spirited natural scientists as well as of alchemists and Illuminati all casting light upon Nature. Maybe the intersection of chemistry and alchemistry helped Victor crucially.

"What manner of creature.might we ourselves together conceive.were such even possible?" How exquisite Zizzi's syntax is! She sounds at least 140 years old to be so cultivated, born in the Age of Manners as well as of Romanticism.

"Conceivably a freak..." And Mengele's ears prick up.

"Yet by what standards, dear Dudu?.by the standards of a Man-Monster?.or by the standards of a Mermaid, me?"

Whereupon Josef gains a more revealing glimpse of the Mermaid bride – and her long swirly light-golden hair triggers a memory from the 1930s!

Back then, Josef is losing his Catholic faith when circumstances cause him to see the wooden altarpiece carved 400 years earlier by famous Bavarian craftsman Tilman Riemenschneider, incorporating the amazing

Ascension of Mary Magdalena up to the Sky. Tilman hails from *Wurst*burg – twisting the name a bit to protect the location, as with *Goonz*burg.

What is amazing is not so much the consummate skill of Riemenschneider in carving the limewood so that the tresses of Mary's lightly golden hair cascade down past her twin naked breasts finally to her groin... no, not Tilman's skill but rather the fact that Mary's entire body – excluding her neck and shoulders and her praying hands and her neat nippled tits – is covered with a natural fur coat of short curly golden hairs.

The story goes that after the crucifixion of the supposed Messiah his admirer Mary, the floozie with faith from the Galilean fishing village of Magdala, spends years in deserts awaiting transport to heaven while angels nourish her by singing. Such is Mary's disdain for mundane things that her garments fall entirely to pieces. To protect her from indecency and from sunburn, since she can't be bothered to get herself a new gown, a coat of curls grows modestly out of her legs and her arms and her trunk. She becomes Hairy Mary.

To Josef this is a particularly ludicrous Roman Catholic myth. He and his comrades ache to liberate German history from Roman and Catholic influences – although when the Führer finally falls those same Romans serve the Nazis well by smuggling hundreds of human monsters from Innsbruck across Italy via chains of obedient monasteries to Rome or to Genoa, whence to South America or Egypt.

And it comes to Josef beholding that altarpiece that *Hairy Mary is a human mutation.* The key to such supposed mysteries, as well as to the making of a master race, is *genetic science* not superstition.

Again, ear-splitting racket erupts. In the sub-tropical trees garish more-than-metre-long macaws flock, their screeches piercing; a bird gotta make itself heard.

Presently the din dies down, leaving only bullfrogs croaking, and Mengele hears in mounting astonishment – supplemented by glimpses – the Man-Monster relating affectionately to the Mermaid further personal history...

"...so on that wee Scots island where nary a sheep grazed and where only a few fisherfolk dwelled – with one cottage conveniently vacant for a fugitive surgeon-scientist such as myself along with that same scientist's lab equipment and his labour-in-progress – and threatened fiercely again by your desperate Dudu with regard to a certain upcoming wedding night of Victor's –"

"– Frankie perforce made use.of what savage Nature.provided –"

"– namely seals of the grey sort, and rowboat-size basking sharks, and hundred-fifty-centimetre fork-tailed salmons and silvery tunas two metres long, and an orca too, thus gainfully employing those aforesaid fisherfolks – including bonny coppery-haired Flora who rested in peace (for a while) in the graveyard of preservative peat after a freak wave snatched her out from the rocky haven where all able-bodied persons struggled to haul a four-tonne female orca ashore – Flora herself never learning to swim since no fatal female should ever go to sea in a fishing boat lest it sink –"

"– thus making myself.a mermaid.of forked silver tail.and freckled bosom, with whom to cross.the briny atlantic deep.in a wooden fishing boat.least worst on the island.leaving some silver thalers behind in more than fair exchange.Shetland-style vessel.cabin on the bow.a cuddy it's called.strong glass bullseye up front.to see through.*Cyclops* you named our boat, my Dudu.who had read books.as I do too now.careful not to make the pages soggy.twin oars for my Dudu to row.hopefully without breaking those oars.due to mighty muscles.cleaving marine resistance –"

"– and lacking stores as well as any larder for stores we feasted upon ocean fish which you caught for us, Zizzy, with your fingernails and your teeth up to a certain size meaning many mackerels and herrings. Flying fish landing within our Sheltie boat best thrown back for being bony and squishy. We ate eels too, and on floating weed we sought crackable suckable crabs –"

What do they do for fresh water to drink? Without which their kidneys must surely fail. What about drinkable water?

Maybe a mermaid has some special adaptation to sea water... But the man-monster too? Mengele is taunted and teased by this enigma. A phantom scalpel quivers in his hand. A propos which, where the devil is his faithful Mauser? Hurled into the river by the explosion of the *Flosshilde*, or else into the jungle...! Yet maybe the Mauser is miraculously close at hand? Josef gropes around between the stray rays of morning light that penetrate between palm fronds. Something he touches clanks.

Immediately a large hole rips open in the patchily mud-plastered wall between hut and house, framing the staring Man-Monster on full alert as well as, partially, the Monster's surprised Mermaid bride.

What happens next is witness to the quickness of Mythic Mengele's mind. Josef gapes approximately towards the noise of demolition as he cries out, "Is somebody there? God help me, somebody! I cannot see! I am blind!" He must *not* focus upon the Monster nor upon the beauteous breasts of the Mermaid, bigger than the titties of demure Hairy Mary but not pumped-up *Playboy*-stupid udders. Josef must not react to anything visible. Lucky indeed that he already glimpsed Monster and Mermaid and isn't excessively shocked by a fuller view. Shutting his eyes, with helplessly questing hands Josef reaches out. "An explosion blinded me. Is somebody there?"

"Explain who you are!" a big voice says.

"I am a doctor... I *was* a doctor before my little steamboat exploded during the storm last night and blinded me. I carry treatments up and down the Paraná to help the tribal people regarding, regarding hookworm and hepatitis and dysentery and typhoid and malaria and TB and Chagas, to help ease their sufferings, for I was fortunate, being qualified as a doctor, to inherit a legacy from an uncle, um, to ease sufferings, which I cannot continue unless my vision returns and oh woe that my surgery with dispensary is a hundred kilometres away downstream, to which how may I return being now blinded?" Should he add, "And maybe also concussed"? That might explain any incoherence in his story. Concussion leads to confusion.

"And maybe concussed," Josef adds, keeping his eyes shut, though careful not to screw them up which would be a reaction to brightness not to darkness.

"Oh one so beneficent to your fellow beings!" Dudu exclaims. "How close to my own heart! In my own modest and discreet way I have helped the autochthonous indigenes of this vast land whose simple wise life of harmony with Nature is assaulted by the lackeys of Kapitalism blazing and bulldozing forests to plant oil palms and to graze beefs until soon enough the soil fails and blows away and the streams are poisoned. How can we not offer you assistance? What say you, my spouse?"

"Oh yes and jawohl," responds Zizzi. "We shall go.a hundred kilometres.with the Doktor.me swimming and fishing.you leading that blind man.along native trails.bewaring of anacondas and jaguars.as well as of any enraged disembowelling Rhea.distant from its preferred dry woodland.cum grassland habitat.the aforementioned Chaco."

Josef can well imagine Zizzi the Mermaid bewaring of anacondas after her own crushing experience. It's impossible to tell whilst pretending to be blind whether her ribs are bruised purple. The dapple of daylight glimpsed earlier was confusing. As for a Rhea, the big flightless bird with its fifteen centimetres claws kicking out like some crazed cassowary may allude to an earlier adventure of herself and Dudu while travelling in the least populated part of Paraguay a century ago, half a century, who can say? Do the pair have any idea what year this is right now? True, they seem informed about economic developments such as deforestation chewing away at their refuges. In secret protection of the savages, has the Monster murdered any intruding cowboys or gold miners or corn oil planters? Briefly Josef shivers at the danger he himself is in. His clothes remain coolly clammy even as the day's heat rises up from the pre-dawn chill. Damn it but he could catch a cold.

Cards played right, the Man-Monster will walk its own way voluntarily right towards Mengele's house and into his laboratory cum surgery! With the Mermaid keeping pace along the Paraná! *Sheer destiny!*

To immobilise this monstrous Tarzan created by Frankenstein, obviously Josef must increase the dose of curare paste which will paralyse a normal human being. He almost certainly lost the jars of curare which were carried on the steamer, but he still has plenty of the dark sticky paste back home on the hacienda. Primitive Amazonians way up north produce the poison for use when hunting with blowpipes. That's much further north than Paraguay, but most things get smuggled into and out of Paraguay across the big sea shining water as the Paraná river is called by some. Guns, fridges, cigarettes, drugs, people. The Pilcomayo River running away westward from Asunción is another useful artery for contraband; while big brother River Paraguay heads north-easterly. But we're on the bigger Paraná further east.

Where is the Doktor's valiant German Shepherdess bitch which was on board *Flosshilde*? Maybe the explosion transformed her into a terrified mongrel cur that ran away. Maybe Brunhilde tumbled dazed into the river for piranhas quickly to deflesh into a skeleton.

A sustaining breakfast before setting out to trek southward! Guided by Dudu's voice alone, Josef steps through the torn-open gap into the humble house. Intentionally stumbling, he dares an eyelids-open glance at his surroundings though not in any co-ordinated way. Zizzi is twisting away waterwards, at once lumbery and limber, like a seal with lady's arms in place of fore-flippers.

Hot embers circled by stones, a few palm logs, a football-size calabash for water, a monster-size matrimonial hammock of netting slung between stakes, assorted rusty utensils, a tottering pile of books blotched by mould. Despite books and matrimonial mattress, this doesn't seem to be any permanent habitation. Mr and Mrs Monster may have similar secret residences scattered across many thousands of square kilometres. The cohabitation of a land dweller and a liquid dweller cannot sustain a perfect home as in US magazines.

"So," asks Dudu, "what brings you originally to the river Paraná, Herr...?"

If Dudu knows about deforestation, might he also be aware of Nazi war criminals? We're in the Sixties. As we said, there are magazines.

"Herr Schmidt. Herr Doktor Schmidt. I come here to help the natives, as I said."

"But why *here* all the way from Süddeutschland?"

Damn this, being interrogated by your destined experimental subject!

"I follow the tradition of Nobel Peace Prize winner Albert Schweitzer." Of whom Josef is aware as a fellow Wagnerian as well as a medical doctor, even though Schweitzer's PhD was in theology.

Within mere minutes the Mermaid returns, a bloodied fish writhing in her jaws opened as wide as possible. Josef identifies in a blink by the black spots all over the grey top and the white belly too, and fins like cherub wings, that it's a surubi catfish, very common and fortunately delicious, not something that tastes of mud. The Doctor's proud of his observational powers and ability to identify things. This surubi's only a cub of a creature; such catfish can get to a metre long and more, forever greedily gorging themselves like eating machines. Dudu bashes the surubi, guts it, wraps it in something rustly, tosses it upon the embers to grill. One might wonder why the Mermaid risks dislocating her jaw, but an unwilling slippery fish could easily escape her hand while swimming and maybe she prefers her mate to deliver the coup de grace.

Before hiking off, there's some of the widely scattered wreckage of *Flosshilde* to confront. Dudu's guidance is surprisingly light upon Josef's shoulder. Dudu carries the smoulder of moss-packed embers in a bark pouch tied to his strong-thonged jaguar loincloth along with other useful things. Those include his gutting and filleting knife and the water-gourd, also snacks such as starch cakes and chipa bread either thieved or received as tribute. Paraguaranís put out little gifts to appease their monsters. Usually rum and cigars, but the giant Man-Monster isn't a naughty shorty like Pombero of the hairy feet who's satisfied with a smoke and booze. Nor is Dudu a hairy short-arse like Kurupi who wraps his prehensile penis around his waist a few times. What our big boy, occasionally glimpsed, needs from time to time is cakes and bread and beef charqui-jerky to supplement fresh fish, fowl, and fruit.

"My bride could report on sunken salvage but I see no way for you to repair your boat. In time to come your timbers may warm our hearth here. Ah, I see a net hurled amongst bushes. A corpse is beneath –"

Tangled, neck broken askew, there's helmsman Enrique amidst dense green. Enrique's assistance will be sorely missed. Where may Alfonso and Tomás be? Thrown elsewhere brokenly? Already eaten by wildlife ranging upward from fire ants to swamp rats and beyond? Alf and Tom's help is essential once they approach closer to the hacienda! Oh destiny, permit at least one of that duo to spy the Man-Monster trampling tamely behind their boss and to put two and two together, zwei und zwei zusammenzählen. Let them not call out like imbeciles, 'Look out behind you, Señor Médico Mengele!'

"You also had a dog?" asks Dudu, and right then Josef daren't risk a blink to see what became of Brunhilde.

"Yes... Did she suffer? No, do not tell me!"

Therefore Dudu doesn't tell. Josef paws at the unseen air like a sign language illiterate. Even if aching for a pee he must never hurry. Pee for prostate, damn it. Wet pants. How unfair that a man of his calibre although of advancing decrepitude... *no no he is Mythic Mengele*, master of deception, luring a distorted Man-Monster back to his lab along with its miscegenating mockery of a mermaid mistress!

Warming puddles remain from the storm on the vague route seemingly chosen at random. The forest respires rainwater, to make for a clammy day, languid, sultry, and tiresome. How many great bony roots has Josef tripped over? Before sundown Zizzi rocks and rolls her way through the dense undergrowth, a drowned teal duck in each hand. Gutting happens, then kindling, then roasting, then ripping up to serve on bits of banana leaf, as is explained patiently to Josef while he sits pretend-blindly where he can do no harm to himself.

Darkness falls. Fireflies flit. Through a rift in the foliage glares a buttery half-moon. No hammocks hereabouts, though no nippy ants either. Mosquitos are a bit of a pest but hereabouts they aren't malarial. Zizzi cuddles up to her beloved minotaur beast. Her Frankentaur. Her Frankenchimera. Vivisections await the pair.

And so to another day, then another day very similar. Rain regularly percolates from the canopy, blurring the vista whenever Josef dares peep, blurring likewise our own view. Endless trees rise from tangles of green and grün and verde vegetation. All the grades of green.

The Mermaid is of course waterproof. Her intermittent visits ashore, squirming and rolling heavily – surprisingly speedily so – make Josef wonder whether the anaconda mistakenly viewed Zizzi as a possible mate, even though Mrs Boa herself was still loaded with a freight of big babies. Can there be such a thing as trans-species tribadism? Can Sapphic bestiality exist? This might be well beyond even Krafft-Ebing's ken as regards perversions.

What a great string of names that sublime sexual expert had! In all its glory: Richard Fridolin Joseph Freiherr Krafft von Festenberg auf Frohnberg, genannt von Ebing! A Free Lord! A Baron appropriately born in *Mann*heim, the Home of Man. Another Josef.

Of a sudden, during a halt for a snack of Kosereva and while the Man-Monster has stepped away to relieve himself amidst shower-curtains of huge leaves, the Sireñorita emits a mixture of girly giggle and gargoyle-like gurgle, as well might a mermaid, then exclaims, "Herr Schmidt, pray why do you.*pretend* to be blind.when this is so inconvenient.for you? Are you hoping.like some spying naturalist.to behold sexual relations.occuring in the boskage?Bestially so.between my wet self.and my big Mensch!"

Damn it but the Herr Doktor feels that he's blushing and flushing due to the grossery – whether innocently or intentionally provocative. Ever since the accident he's been hatless, exposing his brainy forehead, nowhere to hide blushes. To Josef's mind comes a vivid cinematic image of the National Water Corpse, *Reichswasserleicher* Kristina Söderbaum, who in so many movies of the 30s and 40s directed by her Mann Veit Harlan drowns herself after a subhuman besmirches her.

"Or is your pretence of blindness.so that Dudu and I shall serve as bodyguards.and waiters for you.all your way back.to your home?"

What to do, what to say? For a few moments more the candy is glueing Josef's teeth and tongue together; as he duly mimes. Made from sour orange skins and black molasses, chunky Kosereva kind-of-marmalade is bittersweet as well as protein-rich, great for sustaining stamina. Before going for a pee the Man-Monster unstrung from his laden loincloth a clamped airtight jar of Kosereva, suitable for finger extraction being broad and shallow – as Dudu slowly and patiently explained to blind Josef.

Josef swallows all of the sustaining sweetness that's been in his gob. Directly now he gazes into the

Mermaid's liquid eyes rather than in her approximate direction. Improvise! Improvise!

"My dear Fräulein, you discover me!

"You unveil me. You find me out."

Improvise *besser* than that!

"I am ashamed to say that I *bet* drunkenly... with the chef of my ship in our cups... that I could *fool*... the first persons whom I met ashore... by swearing that I couldn't see... but then my boat exploded. Stupidly I became... trapped in consistency."

"Why in Himmel would you bet such a thing?"

"Would that chef be *this person*?" huffs a bearish voice. The Man-Monster emerges from a nearby privy of giant fan-leaves holding aloft by the gathered-up shirt collar the squirming cook Alfonso. Josef cannot believe his luck at this interruption – *or maybe his bad luck?*

Held thus, Alfonso is most prominently a bare belly resembling a barrel cactus, those being alien to hereabouts, sporting a mat of black hair rather than spikes. His heavy brass belt-buckle tries to drag his jeans kneewards. A past Christmas gift of caprice from his employer, the buckle brags *Mercedes Benz Germany*.

"Wretch, you were spying upon me while I pissed!" Dudu accuses the dangled cook in Deutsch, assuming at least this much relationship with the enigmatic Herr Schmidt. Why else would this walking belly be skulking here in the bushes? Unless he's some innocent tribespeasant passing by... "Forgive my frank language, beloved!"

Alfonso cries out in Spanish, "I have hunger, Jefe –"

Josef invariably addresses his cook and other employers and workers in Spanish passable due to years in South America, though he only smatters in Portuguese. But is Alfonso appealing now to Josef – or to his captor?

Switching to Spanish, Dudu growls, "What kind of hunger would that be?" *Qué tipo de hambre* and so on.

"How sweetly sour the Kosereva smells –!" Alfonso's nostrils must be much sensitised by a grumbling tummy.

With his clean left hand Josef is still gripping the jar half-full of the sticky stuff. The cook may well have been trailing after them simply in order to feed on their abandoned daily left-overs.

"Wait a minute!" Dudu booms at the Death Doctor. "Did you really recover your sight just now in a medical miracle? Or did you *tell a lie to us* about being blind?"

Urgently Josef jerks the jar towards Alfonso. "Chef, remember my bet with you that I can pretend to be blind!? Me, Herr Schmidt!?"

Josef daren't of course resort to winking. However, times enough Alfonso has successfully bargained with smugglers, consequently the cook isn't slow-witted. Not to mention keeping the pantry at the hacienda well stocked without being swindled. The cook isn't from a degenerate slave race such as the Slavs.

Josef cries out with a great show of distress, "Are you aware, oh Alfonso, that poor Enrique lost his life in the explosion of our boat? And is Tomás anywhere to be seen? – I mean seen by persons not pretending to be blind?"

Confused, Dudu finally lowers Alfonso to stand on his own, still restrained by the collar of his checked red shirt. The cook pays scant heed to the pink-nippled breasts of the mermaid, salivating instead at sight of the jam-jar with its remains of marmalade peel in molasses. For the moment Alfonso favours flavours above all else. Fingerlicking Kosereva confiture. If one were a looming Man-Monster, one might feel almost insulted by inattention.

On the second morning of the journey Josef realised that the mermaid's nipples never shrank nor do they shrink. This may slightly reduce her streamlining in the water but enhances her sex appeal. Does Josef recall correctly that zoologically a lady seal's nipples are fully retractable?

Concentrate! Agitating the jam-jar, Josef demands of his employee, "Well?"

"Yes. Blind. Well. Yes. Herr Schmidt."

"Indeed Herr Dudu, I can fully confirm that this is my chef Alfonso." Unlocked from sightless immobility, Josef hastens forth to thrust the jar into his cook's eager hands. "Alfonso," he murmurs, "do you happen to have any cigarettes?"

"If so, I'd have chewed them all by now," as the chef's forefinger hooks into the confiture.

"I'm not sure this is a satisfactory explanation," Zizzi protests.

So as to retain the initiative for a short while longer, Josef makes a megaphone of his hands and shouts into the tangled forest, "Tomás! Tomás! Tomás!" How unlikely that Tomás is sneaking after his compañero Alfonso in the same way that Alfonso was tailing the trio of Man-Monster, Mermaid, and Mengele.

Thus far on these faint forest paths trodden by mixed-breed persons and savage wild pigs they've encountered nobody else. Does the world hold its breath as they pass by? Yea valuably so in the case of the pioneering duo of elder refugees from Europe! No, let's make that a *trio* of refugees, ill-assorted. Nothing that is South American especially wishes to investigate them. Doktor Mengele benefits from local incuriosity, corruption, and incompetence, and will continue to do so – up until his forthcoming devoutly-to-be-wished scientific vindication and social rehabilitation which dissected Dudu and Zizzi will provide.

In view of Alfonso's finger-licking show of starving – all be it belied by the cook's belly – Dudu charitably issues him some sun-dried beef to chew. If only, reflects Mengele, the Mermaid were a marsupial gifted with a waterproof pouch for carrying groceries. Can a kangaroo-style pouch possibly be constructed surgically for the Sireñorita from existing tissue?

Zizzi rears her flaxen-haired head and her bosoms up high, figurehead-like, and declares, "Herr Schmidt.since you can see.quite clearly.from which I request you.to desist as regards myself.our ways may now part!"

Spoken without consulting Dudu – easy to guess who wears the trousers in *her* miscegenating ménage. Immediately Mengele panics at the prospect of imminent sudden separation from Monster and Mermaid.

"Please, no, Fräulein, I beg you! This dummkopf cook and I are sure to take a wrong route!" Josef speaks in German in case Alfonso contradicts him, helpfully. "It's *ein hundert* kilometres through jungle wilderness."

"Surely seventy by now," Zizzi observes reasonably. "Simply keep the river to your left. Do not wander far from the Big-Sea water."

Josef tries again. "Alas I have not been paying proper attention to our surroundings due to myselbst acting consistently with blindness. I am only used to travel by boat, not by boots. The cook, he could only think of trailing after us like a stray dog sniffing for scraps." Like the semi-starved strays that follow Josef around the hacienda, no those are powerful muscular Alsation Shepherds and sleek speedy black Dobermanns.

"You can rest and recuperate at my home, Fräulein and Mighty Mensch, unless you have some urgent destination in a different direction. Pardon my impertinence, Fräulein, but may I presume that you yourself need to stay close to water? At my home I have a big bath to put at your disposal." Via which, blood can drain away not to be wasted but to be piped to a pig trough.

At this moment from further along the trail an unseen pigeon or two throb deeply:

'*WhoCooksYou? WhoCooksYou?*'

Dudu raises a hefty hand to silence those present. But the Mermaid declares, "Mein Liebling.I fear that Mennonites.have colonised here.since last we passed by."

"Mennonites!"

"How else can there be *pigeons*?"

"What exactly," queries Mengele, "is wrong with Mennonites? At least they speak a sort of German. They keep to themselves. They work hard."

"Ach yes they work *hard* at destroying the forest!" rages the Man-Monster. "Hard at tearing out hundreds of hectares of heartland, ripping out the stumps and roots. Putting *peanuts* everywhere in place of the wondrous web of Nature! Destroying den wunderbar Wald! I piss on their pathetic Jesus and his groundnuts! And where earthnuts are – can *pigeons* be far behind? Come along, let us behold what natural disaster will appal our eyes! Let us follow the song of the Picazuró Pigeon!"

Josef struggles to avoid speaking out more fulsomely in favour of Mennonites, eighty per cent of whom would have gone 'home to the Reich' in response to the Führer's invitation, this invitation being urged on them due to their Aryan purity, greater even than some members of the SS. Later, how well placed in Paraguay are the Mennonites when the time comes to hide Nazis absconding from Europe. Throughout the blundering hunt for Doktor Mengele how nicely the Mennonites distract attention geographically away towards the Chaco region – from which they are now extending their settlements, verdammt!

"Brochettas de paloma," Alfonso murmurs wistfully as his hands skewer imaginary pigeon breasts. Better than boiling tough parrots for half a day.

Abrupt as a precipice, sudden as a crevasse in a glacier, fatal as a fault line in the fabric of reality, the dense forest ceases. A big though bounded plain opens out ahead, shaved clear with absolute precision of all trees as well as of subordinate vines and vegetation. In place of Nature, almost to the limits of vision tens of thousands of monotonous little clumps of foliage lie upside-down, drying or dying, their torn-up nodulous roots poking towards the sky. Well no, not quite to the limit of sight. This illusion of immensity is due to spending several days in dense jungle with nothing by way of deep distances.

The usual world is inverted indeed. The double-pods of peanuts always develop underneath the soil, their pretty flowers pushing pegs down into the ground below them to ensure this. As Dudu and Zizzi and Josef and Alfonso emerge on to the margin of this devastation, hundreds of pigeons take wing from the peanut plants which obviously were not upturned by pea-brained pigeons but rather by... Still within sight are the straw hats and plain calico dresses of the departing upturner women – who surely cannot permit such losses of their crop to a crowd of aerial pests, unless the Mennonite Messiah advocates a major turning of the cheek for the sake of commensality, as if pigeons and sparrows should peck upon the table of Leonardo's *Last Supper* sharing unrisen bread with the disciples.

'Crop' here refers to the farmers' crop of produce rather than to the muscular oesophagal pouches of pigeons into which the fat birds cram the surplus of what they peck up. This may be clearer in Deutsch: the farmer's *Frucht* goes into the pigeon's *Kropf*.

These Mennonites are metastasizing far from where they first began up in the high dry northerly Chaco. How have they come a-colonising here so far south-by-east? A surviving windbreak of primal forest lets vague shapes of buildings show through its curtain, hints of a tame tidy toy town that's beginning to show lighted windows. These farmers very likely also plant lots of cotton on other denuded and raped virgin land nearby for self-sufficient prosperity.

Fifty pigeons take panicky flight – for now a pair of lanky adolescents dressed in calico shirts and denim are emerging from the surviving forest, each of them toting a kerosine lantern and what looks like an old long barrel shotgun. Dusk is gloaming fast. The unfull moon has yet to rise.

Mennonites are pacifists, never in fact heeding Adolf's call of return to the Nazi Reich. However, given the Mennonites' bygone inclinations towards the Fatherland, the presence of a few shotguns among these pacifists is... well, frankly it's peanuts.

The couple of hicks discharge their shotguns towards the airborne pigeons. Now that the frauleins have safely gone let's have some birds for the pot! A dozen fat pigeons tumble out of the wheeling flock that's heading for safety in the nearest part of the straight wall of trees surrounding the vast clearing. This sort of barrel-chested pigeon prefers to roost in trees after pecking about on open spaces. Such pigeons simply shouldn't be *here at all* way down upon the Paraná river except that the multiplying Mennonites are now carving out the perfect combination of terrain for these palomas.

Already the hicks are reloading when FrankenDudu roars the revenge of the jungla. Across that field the Man-Monster charges. He leaps over rows of inverted groundnuts, uttering a curdling outcry. One of the Hicks, call him Heinz – 'he who rules the roost, or the household' – has time to shoot at the oncoming malformed looming menace although surely no savage psycho gorilla apemen roam the junglas of Paraguay! Yet this might be one of those Guaraní or Tupí monsters, not so mythic now, are they? Squealing, Dudu throws up a mighty mitt all too late. Shutgun pellets have bloodied and blinded his left eye while other pellets pock and pit his flesh.

Dudu's right eye still sees. Heinz is swatted aside, as is his brother or inbred cousin who may well (or ill) be called Hacken, butcher of trees. Then the injured Man-Monster gathers up one of the fallen shotguns. With supernal strength he bends the twin steel barrels around

Heinz's neck, almost making a lazo or crude ampersand shape. This done, he wraps Hacken's neck likewise with the other shotgun although less tightly. After thrashing briefly, Heinz may already have expired due to the pressure upon his carotids or his jugulars, or both. Desperately Hacken tries to force his fingers within the noose of steel.

Dudu rocks backwards in renewed discomfort. How much pain can Dudu feel? Presumably he experiences pleasures such as Zizzi also enjoys when he copulates with her cloaca. If pleasure comes, can pain be far behind?

Maybe it was a bad auspice to baptise their Scottish boat 'Cyclops'... if an auspice might apply a century and a half *before* the event which is auspiced! Let's not forget that 'auspice' originally refers to the patterns of birds in flight – and pigeons have just flown, fatally for some of them.

Enough about pigeons and peanuts of Paraguay! Enough.

In the dusk Zizzi may not notice any damage done to Dudu, which may yet turn out to be trivial. The Monster-Man has redoubtable recuperative powers. Careful not to conceal his injured eye ostentateously and thus alarm Zizzi, Dudu returns at Olympic hurdler pace over the rows of pulled-up peanut plants.

"My love," she calls out to him from amidst crushed bushes, "have you purged.your justifiable rage?

If so, despite the light dying.we should move away from this.this Mennonightmare."

Dudu chortles at her drollery since him chortling reassures Zizzi.

And thus they all move onward together, the Mermaid now gripped in Dudu's muscular arms gazing backward as rearguard along their route. When Heinz and Hacken bring back no pigeons surely Mennonite men must set out to investigate. All the sooner if Hacken staggers back in to Toy Town wearing the twisted gun as a necktie. Babbling chokedly, one hopes, of a bizarre Guaraní or Tupí myth-beast much bigger than any savage warped piggy or sheepy thing.

Three

We must suppose that Dudu spends the night in some discomfort due to his injuries by pellets, nevertheless he resolutely spoons and cuddles Zizzy upon the foliage of the forest floor, as is his manner. Now it's a sweltering misty musty morning.

Zizzi was stitched together from parts of previously cool-blooded and previously warm-blooded creatures. A blubbery seal is warm whereas a cod is a cool customer. In a subtropical clime Zizzi may experience shivers at the same time as hot flushes. Cuddling evens out her slumbers.

Zizzy wriggles deeper into privacy while birds and monkeys chatter crazily to greet the day. Dudu shifts alongside the Doktor and insists, "Kindly look into my left eye."

"Hmm... Ach... So... you were hit by a Schrot or by several from that boy's Schrotshooter."

"And now I cannot see at all on the left! I assure you that I do not parody your previous pretence of blindness!"

"By no means, by no means."

Oh blessings, oh fortunate fate for Josef.

"I may need a doctor or a surgeon to *do* something."

"I am both, oh Benefactor," declares Doktor Schmidt.

"Do I need a bandage around my brow?"

"With the loss of my boat," declares Josef, "the only available scalpels and stitch-needles and surgical tweezers and magnifiers and all else are back at my residence. We must hurry there as quickly as possible. This is urgent because you have ocular trauma with hyphema. You have double penetration and or perforation of the globe. Intraocular haemorrhage. Maybe detachment of the retina. Let us send Alphonso trotting ahead to prepare my surgery for your arrival. At the moment the best first aid, as you correctly guess, is a clean rag or perhaps big leaves using vines as twine to protect the site of trauma *without touching* the eyeball itself. To cover both eyes, thus to forestall automatic coupled movements is ideal, yet this may slow us to a snail's pace, perhaps disastrously for your vision."

"I can ride upon my bride's back while she swims swiftly along with the current –"

Verdammt. "But then your surgeon-doctor cannot accompany you. Just in case your eye has a crisis."

"Why not? Buoyed by the water, you will weigh less. My bride has a firm back and strong spine."

Bitterly to Josef's mind comes the remembrance of himself blithely humming so recently *Siegfried's Journey Down the Rhine.*

"Is your bride not slippery? I may slide off her."

"I will hold you tight."

This is becoming intolerable. They will look like naval frogmen riding a torpedo with a female figurehead.

"Piranhas or dorados may bite my legs. Do they not sometimes bite yours –?" Ach, but don't forget about the protective stench released by her cloaca... presumably! To which the Man-Monster is oblivious and maybe Josef too come to think of it. So far Josef has noticed nothing nasally offensive. Zizzi's cloaca may need stimulation to produce a protective odour. Alternatively, she is very unlike an anaconda. Only dissection can tell for sure.

The disadvantage of arriving unannounced at the hacienda is that the housekeeper cum washerwoman Beatrix – who hails from tiny Bella Vista in north-east Paraguay directly adjacent to Brazil's corresponding Bela Vista with one 'l' – will not expect the advent of a Man-Monster accompanied by a Mermaid even if the good *Doktor Schmidt*, collector of anatomical specimens, accompanies those two.

("I come home so soon, Beatrix! Yes it's me, Doktor SCHMIDT. SCHMIDT – don't you remember my name, eh? Ha ha." Josef does his best to teach Beatrix and Alfonso and Tomás the tricky Bavarian card game of Sheep's Head, widely regarded as a supreme mental discipline. "Silly Beatrix, without your glasses don't you recognise a *Schmidt* when you see one?" Doubtless fifteen mongrel dogs will have no such problem and will be yapping and whining for scraps.)

As soon as Zizzi shows up again, Dudu presents to her his ravaged countenance. "Alas my love, my rage of yestereve made me at least temporarily lose the light of one eye due to Schrots from the Schrotshooter. Yet Doctor Schmidt assures me that his surgery is well equipped and himself a surgeon. All may be well *provided we reach there quickly*."

Zizzi gazes into Dudu's bloodily injured eyeball. "Are you hurting much.my Treasure?" How brave to cuddle all night long while his eye ached and bled within.

Alfonso is already making himself useful finding some big leaves lacking toxic sap or glue or itchy hairs or other inconveniences common to Paraguayan vegetation. Plus he finds some non-toxic lengths of vine to serve as twine to tie the leaves in position around Dudu's forehead. Frankly, reflects Josef, FrankenDudu's passion for raw nature as opposed to neat Germanic farms is sentimental in the extreme. Raw nature in these sub-tropics is so often an impenetrable tangle of thorns and traps and webs and toxicity and humid rot along with ambush by fire ants and by shrieking bullet ants behaving like screaming Stukas, and by carnivorous burrowing bot flies and bloodsucker cone-noses and dengue mosquitoes and black widows and pit vipers and lanceheads and fiery chili pepper tarantulas. What's more, given all the warm humidity and the rich humus of decay, it's a wonder that this trail they're following isn't already wholly overgrown.

As Mengele dresses the injured eye professionally...

"Liebchen, do you suppose that the doctor and I may both ride upon you down the river, so as to arrive the sooner at his surgery?" With its nickel taps and its marble dissecting table just the same as back at Auschwitz.

Is the Sireñorita taken aback? She considers.

"So who will sit in front.and who behind?"

"I must sit behind," says Dudu, "so as to stabilise the doctor."

"But then his knees.may nudge my bosoms."

Dudu's big hands conjure anatomy in mid-air. "Not necessarily, my love."

"His feet.may touch.my tits," says Zizzi more crudely, the better to make her point. Her Man-Monster was created so innocent originally. "Assuming," continues the Sireñorita, "that the doctor.first removes his shoes.and ties those around his neck."

"What if he pulls up his knees like a jockey does?" Dudu once spied on a horse race from a bushy hillside.

"Raise his knees," enquires his bride, "without *stirrups*.to rest his feet in?"

Twin feet are something of a mystery to Zizzi who has a tail, all be it forked, upon which she can never walk nor waddle. Yet with sufficiently clever surgery by employing metal rods, can her skeleton be reinforced? Can her tail be split into two, like the separation of conjoined Siamese twins? Indeed, is her broad and beautiful tail sustained by bone – or by cartilage? Might her tail be like a ray's wing which can be floured and fried in butter, a fish knife then scraping the luscious pink flesh off in strings? Beware that this passing flash of culinary phantasie does not divert from scientific duties!

Practical Alfonso butts in: "I'm sure I can contrive a saddle and girth plus straps using vines and lianas. I did retain a pocket knife in my pocket."

"Um," from Josef, "how long will a suitable saddle and girth take to make?"

Zizzi bridles at this. "Surely I shall not.be ridden.like a mare! Nor shall I be fitted.by a cook.for a corset!" Zizzi is aware of corsets due to damp fashion magazines glanced through over the years.

"How long, my Alfonso? Ich, Doctor *Schmidt* need to know. Time is of the essence."

"Maybe two hours, maybe three... Liana vines can be tough to cut through."

"All the while our Benefactor's eye worsens!"

"All the while," says Zizzi," those oh so pacifistic Mennonite.menschen may set out in pursuit.with pitchforks.to avenge the strangulation.of their son with a shotgun. Unless they worry.what sort of creature.can bend steel gun barrels.like rubber... We ought to proceed.forthwith on foot. And fin."

Does she mean 'fin' in the sense of an *end* to any further debate? Or is she alluding ironically to her own anatomy, to her mighty Schwimmflosse? In which case, how urgent does she truly treat the diagnosis and repair of her Beloved's eye as being? Or wait, *may* she suspiciously be testing Josef to measure his reactions? Mermaids are known for their wiles.

Mermaids, plural? In the real world there is only *one* mermaid, *singular*, the work of Victor Frankenstein, great flawed genius of mankind. All other mermaids are mere mythology.

Relapsing for a moment from the mythic into the mundane, Josef Mengele feels such desperate craving for a ciggy.

Due to the Sireñorita's ambivalence regarding being ridden upon by anyone beyond her Beloved, they now move onward separately. Zizzy resorts on her own to the Big Sea river; the Paraná still remains within yodeling distance. Bandaged in green, Dudu leads one-eyed along a faint land route, followed by the Doctor, Alfonso the cook bringing up the rear.

They cover a couple of kilometres on a track reverting to the wild. By now the Sireñorita must have covered about a thousand horizontal fathoms – when a steep-sided stream wide as three Dudus stretched out foot to shoulder interrupts their way. A tree has fallen from this side across to the further bank. Maybe a quinine tree? The trunk looks wide enough to wobble across with care. Hopefully not hiding horror-thorns if it isn't benign quinine. The narrow bridge is green with mosses and ferns. Offering a soft, or a slippery, transit? Vines, which may have choked the tree to death till it tumbled, dangle in the water.

"Beloved-ay-eee-ooo!" yodels Dudu. Recall that he was brought into being in Bavaria. "Crossing little river on tree-Ay-Ee-Oooo!" he yodels again, mounting with mighty feet the greened trunk, slippy-sliding though immediately recovering his balance.

"Verstanden-ay-ee-ooo," comes a muted response from the direction of the Paraná, much vegetation being in between but audible nonetheless.

Next, Josef mounts the tree-bridge and for the first time fully observes at close quarters Dudu's bullish cum equine back corded with musculature, ripe for dissection dead or alive. Lastly comes Alfonso – though oops down slips the cook heavily to bestride the mossy trunk cowboy-style, jolting his pouch of procreation; a great yelp is followed by groans.

"Stay-ee-ooo there.a while to speak.Dudu-ee-ooo!" What does Zizzi want to sprechen about? Something unforeseen, noticed by her further downstream? Obediently Dudu pauses above the midstream of this fairly piddling though by no means negligible tributary. Behind Dudu, Josef balances, swaying. Alfonso shuffles along silently, using the tree as a saddle, favouring his aching balls; obviously he's a guy *con cojones*.

Of a sudden the stream fizzles and bubbles with a panic of piranhas, not just the red-belly sort but black-bodies too all mixed up in confusion. The oncoming mermaid is effectively herding the carnivorous fishes which react in threat and alarm by barking and gnashing their teeth – not nearly as noisily as would a dog bark or gnash, unless one is a fish underwater endowed with a swim-bladder. Now here comes Sireñorita Zizzi herself cutting through their shoals, her mighty splashing and tail-lashing parting piranhas to right and to left. How the water heaves, releasing bitter odours from the weeds that fringe it.

Almost inexplicably a South-Deutsch yodel rings out from the *rear* of Dudu, Doctor, and cook. *"[Unclear] ay-ee-ooo! [Unclear] He-ho!ay-ee-ooo!"*

And this is also when from behind bushes *ahead* beyond the tree trunk bridge arise handyman Tomás and at least ten Tupí tribespersons.

What's more, moments later banging from those bushes suddenly soars the net meant to catch a mermaid, taking flight across the tributary.

It takes no great genius to deduce that Tomás sought sanctuary with extended family after the *Flosshilde* exploded and that Tomás induced those pureblood natives by the promise of money from Mengele to recover the net and the firing tubes and reload those with undamp powder and to hasten ahead of Dudu's party being slowed by Josef's pretence of blindness, to set up an ambush at a crucial point in the trail.

Emerging from the route which Dudu's party already used, come calico-shirted straw-hatted newcomers sporting blue jeans enlarging that route with sickles and scythes and some swift sawing. Also brandishing pitchforks and hoes.

A mob of Mennonites! Identical blond-headed male ranks collide as they halt. The spectacle before them is too complex to comprehend quickly, especially for the meek in mind.

Tomás bellows proudly, "Boss, I catch your specimens for the slab! This two'll cut up nice!"

The net sinks down upon Dudu, upon Josef, then on the cook seated on the trunk as well as upon Zizzy who is now rearing from the water to reach her Beloved. She's like a colossal salmon encountering a weir on her way upstream to spawn; and she hears very clearly what Tomás bellows.

"¡Bien, Tomás! Sehr Gut!" calls out Josef through the net. "But use no curare!" Just in case someone is over-enthusiastic. No premature deaths.

Many tribespersons call out, "We jump to meet you!" This is how you greet a person in Tupí: "I jump to meet you!" How appropriate, what with Zizzy leaping yet falling back as a salmon might at a weir, with a vast splash that frenzies the piranhas...

"Beware tooth-fishes!" comes a cry in Tupí.

... only for Zizzi to launch herself once again like a missile from a nuclear submarine, this time successfully.

Loosely netted, Zizzy crashes upon the log bridge, and it isn't so much the additional weight of the mermaid as the kinetic energy of her impact which cracks the long log, KRACHEN! Tangled in netting, its occupants all slide towards the water. Powerfully Dudu turns to drag himself upward again. This lifts the net enough to let Josef escape, inhale, and dive underwater, dolphin-kicking upstream a few metres till he can grip roots of the bank and haul himself out, on the Tupí side.

As Dudu rises up once more into full view of the tribespersons it's evident that Tomás may not have explained the whole situation clearly enough. Some of those tribespersons seem to imagine that in FrankenDudu they're encountering one of their own traditional monsters which typically roam woodlands, whereupon they nock arrows.

Or else the Tupís are reacting to the sight also confronting them of a small army of Mennonites weaponed agriculturally...

Or a bit of both.

Arrows fly. A tall Mennonite cries out and collapses.

Terribly, one of the arrows goes into Dudu's eye, provoking a hideous howl of pain. And of near-despair – since now Dudu is double-blinded. Oh dark dark dark, total eclipse for Dudu. Now he's unable to see what others can see. For just now the morning mists clear and the sun pierces through, here where this minor river opens a rift up to the forest canopy – and a faint rainbow arches briefly above the broken tree-bridge above the water; which mythic Mengele certainly sees so that he hums the rainbow Leitmotif from *Das Rheingold*. More grandly in keeping with Mengele's rank of Hauptsturmführer, 'Hauptmotif' is what Wagner vainly hoped that these musical phrases might be called. High rank is important.

Actually, Dudu's pelleted left eye does still display curdled light, but that's pretty useless. If the lovers can escape from this mess, may a mermaid conceivably lead her blinded Beloved about like some kind of Samson instead of a one-eyed Wotan? Can she herself be borne by him while from her enhanced elevation as of a giantess she surveys which way to walk and duly directs her SamsonDudu?

The Mennonite men's only shotguns must be those back at their township tied into loops. So therefore from their front rank a sickle hurtles, rotating as it rushes through the air. Then another sickle.

Oh terrible happenstance, oh fatal fortunity, one strong sharp blade curves itself around Dudu's neck. Before tumbling into the stream the sickle slices both a carotid artery *and* a jugular vein – there's such a bursting forth of orange-blue blood... as Dudu falls down amid the shoal of crazed piranhas.

Whatever the Sireñorita meant to sprechen earlier on is now completely moot. From the bank, Death-Doctor Mengele SS PhD PhD surveys the ruin of his hopes. Zizzi spies him there and she knows him for what he is and understands his frustrated intentions towards her. Such hatred for a man in a mermaid's eyes has never before been seen.

Twisting, the Sireñorita slips free of the net, plunging into the bloodied water to try to haul away to some kind of safety her fast-succumbing, futilely flailing Beloved from amidst the tooth-fishes feeding upon him. To a certain extent she succeeds – Dudu's body does move away downstream in the current, followed by hungry fishes, forever to be beyond Josef's reach.

Just as he himself might be well advised to relocate himself well beyond the retributive reach of the Sireñorita.

Unlike mythic Mengele, mundane Mengele hasn't been at any place in Paraguay since October 1960. Josef becomes paranoid after the Israelis kidnap Eichmann, so he moves to Brazil.

Time passes. A decade and more disappears. For thirteen years Mengele stays with a family of neo-Nazis called the Stammers in Nova Europa, Brazil, managing a coffee and cattle farm. Nova Europa is nicely isolated over three hundred kilometres north-west of São Paolo, and 20 kilometres from the Tielê tributary of the Paraná – could well be further from the river system, but surely no mermaid can crawl across 20 kilometres of dry heat.

The family name 'Stammers' doesn't mean that the Stammers stottern. It takes the Stammers a long while finally to fall out with ever-whining, sharp-tempered, quarrelsome, chain-smoking Mengele. His moods fluctuate wildly. He does accomplish some water-skiing locally in company with an ex-Nazi flying ace.

More years pass by. Very occasionally an implausible report appears in newspapers about a mermaid sighted swimming in the Paraná or in the rivers Paraguay or Uruguay or in the Iguaçu or in the Tietê or in the Negro or in the Pilcomayo river and or in the hundred-kilometre wide muddy estuary of Río de la Plata.

Doubtless that's a manatee alias sea cow somehow gone astray from the Amazon up north.

Spurious sightings of Mengele 'last week' or 'last month' come far more frequently and are believed enthusiastically. A totally wrong photo of an alleged Mengele continues to circulate everywhere.

Chronologically contradicting Josef's supposed thirteen years with the Stammers, in 1969 he moves to within 40 kilometres of vast subtropical São Paulo to reside with better quality hosts. Absolute accuracy is futile as we teeter on a rainbow bridge between the mundane and the mythic.

Time passes, till the white-haired Doctor cum Handyman sporting a Nietszschean moustache becomes totally alone, in a yellow stucco bungalow in a slum area of the Eldorado suburb of São Paulo, specifically number 5555 along dusty pot-holed everlasting Avarenga Road – eat your hearts out, Mossad, for that address. Wiesenthal pinpoints mythic Mengele way up the Paraná bordering Argentina where fair-haired Nazi bigots live in Bavarian-style chalets, this area being 'New

Bavaria'. A certain Judge Chichizola of Peru affirms that a visit by Meng the Merciless to his own nation is *indisputable*. They seek him here, they seek him there.

Afflicted with gloom, mundane Mengele thinks about suicide, but someone steals his Mauser. He pays hush-money to somebody else. His right hand trembles due to a stroke recovered from. Illnesses and afflictions assail him. Everything seems empty. But wait! After years of planning, in coordination with what we discreetly refer to as homebase Goonzburg, which knows exactly where the most-sought war criminal is, in September 1977 Josef's son Rolf is on his way to visit his decaying dad on a charter flight from Luxemburg. Since Dad manifests no remorse nor guilt whatsoever for being Meng the Merciless, more modern-minded Rolf's visit isn't exactly a success... except in the sense that nobody notices the son of the Most Sought being present in Brazil.

By the next year Josef loses the will to live and the southerly summer is sweltering. Yet a stay at the seaside might cheer him up. Specifically, at beachside Bertioga a couple of hours by bus from vast São Paulo, where the Bosserts rent a holiday bungalow. That's Wolfram Bossert and Liselotte, plus kids Andreas and Sabine. The Neo-Nazi 'Wolf-Raven' father is fond of klassikal musik and supplies kasettes to Josef. As for Liselotte, nice Nazi wives such as herself rarely realise that their Christian name is half-Hebrew.

Variously along its five beaches Bertioga boasts wide flat white sands and palm trees as well as giant slabs of rock lapped by a gentle Atlantic, although beware of strong currents. A previous German visitor to the area, with a great forked golden beard, captured by cannibals, survived to publish in 1557 his international best-seller *True Story and Description of a Country of Wild, Naked, Grim, Man-eating People in the New World.*

It's February 7th, 1979, about 4.00 in the afternoon, when Josef enters the ocean and wades out to swim-depth. We believe he has no intention of drowning himself.

After a while he feels himself suddenly tugged beneath the surface – yet not by any undercurrent. By a strong hand; he's being held firmly. A face confronts him underwater. Her gaze locks upon his. The colour of her eyes is a lovely liquid aqua. It's almost the same hue as the blue dye he injected into the irises of brown-eyed gypsy girls, causing painful infections, often blinding the kids. Were the Mermaid's eyes really brilliant blue when last he saw her? Dammit but Josef was never quite close enough to her. He was waiting for the intimacy of the operating table. Now she's right in his face, as if about to give him mouth-to-mouth. Is she going to plant her lips upon his lips to suck and blow while twisting his nose shut? So that by slowly measuring out the respiration she might extend his suffering? No, she's only taunting him. She won't sully her lips.

Effortlessly she keeps him just underwater. How does he not remember perfectly the colour of her eyes?

A trough in the water exposes his whole head for some moments – and hers too, her oily lank lightly golden hair reminding him of that carving done by Tilman.

Smiling, she slides Josef underneath the trough as it passes over. Only his arm breaks surface unseen, to wave desperately at anyone, clawing the air to no avail.

Confronting Josef is a Mermaid in whom beasts and sea beasts and human beings mingle, no mutation but a triumph of surgery. How can she possibly have found him? When all the other seekers failed? Mossad, the CIA, the FBI, the Federal German Government, Simon Wiesenthal... seekers with far more resources and mobility than a mermaid confined to watercourses and to the ocean. Can she sense the faintest of scents in water, such as lure an eel across a whole ocean, a salmon across a whole sea and up a river leap by leap almost to the source?

Years of search! Yet here she is, face to face with Josef underwater, keeping both of their faces just under the surface as his eyes flutter and his face tingles and he feels himself impossibly spinning. A lightning bolt of pain shafts through his head and he realises that a stroke has struck him just as happened three years earlier when *that* particular cerebral haemorrhage was classified as mild... except that back then he was standing beside the gate to his bungalow in Alvarenga Road, but now he's way out of his depth, the doll of a mermaid.

The cork pops to the surface. Visibly the swimmer is in distress. Wolfram Bossert rushes to the aid of Josef who briefly seems to rally but then all the power goes out of him. Not quite the Man of Tungsten Steel, Wolfram Bossert nearly kills himself dragging the corpse ashore, exhausted; though at least half a cigar to him for effort and dedication.

The body lies around on the beach for quite a while. As darkness falls, Liselotte holds a lit candle to Josef, lamenting loudly, "The Uncle is dead!"

Der Onkel ist tot! It's a long while since the Uncle wore on his rakishly tilted SS cap the totenkopf, the death's head badge. Ethnic victim children in Auschwitz also used to call Josef 'Uncle' because he grinned and gave them sweeties a few days before he experimented on them strapped down without anaesthetic. From time to time his corpse is moved further upshore to keep it ahead of the tide.

Sightings of mythic Mengele continue for years. Jaw-dropping rewards are offered. Hysterical manhunts happen.

Zizzi's revenge is fulfilled. As long as the agent of Dudu's death survived, Dudu stayed hauntingly present. Now Zizzy needs a new purpose.

A bit later in big Brazil, as well as elsewhere around the world, the funeral flames of the planet will burn in a Götterdammerung of destruction by godlike and mundane Homosaps alike, in a Wagnerian demise of humans greedily multiplying, armed with mighty mincing machines. As if from a Valhalla in flames, smoke will hide the sun. Where, any more, may a long-living mermaid safely swim?

After snacking on oily mackerel, Zizzi tunes her siren-senses. Faintly a flavour from afar brings a hint of sunken Atlantis and aquamen – yet this particular current may suck her from out of Reality into Mythical realms. On the contrary, Zizzi strongly asserts her authenticity.

Epilogue

She's the creation of anatomical artifice and alchemy. The future world, blasted and burned and buffeted, may only be suitable for artificial beings. Right now surely some scientific genius akin to Victor Frankenstein is developing an android superior to Homosap which will survive and reproduce along with superior femoids – maybe to live underwater, protected from the super-storms above, from the floods and from forever droughts, from all the fatal unravelling of habitats. Zizzi has read many damp magazines while resting during her odyssey.

Japan must be where to go. Due to all its mountains important things in Japan are often close to the sea where a mermaid may slip ashore, or even wait for a tsunami to give her a lift further inland.

From here off the coast of Brazil, Japan is further than she ever dreamt of swimming. Yet a swim across half the globe begins with a single stroke.

[With thanks as promised to enthusiastic amis in Amiens]

About the Author

Ian Watson moved to leafy Asturias half way along the top of Spain 10 years ago when he and supertranslator, author, and festival director Cristina Macía married. They organised the 2016 European SF Convention right in the beating heart of Barcelona. Best Souvenir Book ever! Also published that year was Ian's most recent story collection, *The 1000 Year Reich* (NewCon Press), 'Reich' as in Wilhelm Reich the orgone sex therapist. A merry 'spacetime opera' and a jaunty 'spacetime pantomime' appeared in 2016 and 2019 (from PS), entitled *The Brain From Beyond* and *The Trouble With Tall Ones*. A grand finale is threatened, the 'spacetime melodrama' *Mayhem on the Moon*. For their 50th anniversary, Spain's biggest book club invited Cristina and Ian to collaborate on a colourful historical cookbook, *50 recetas con nombre*, collecting 50 dishes bearing the names of persons such as Parmentier Potatoes. Ian's favourite food is Gulas fried with garlic and peppers. (These are sea-worms, not a typo for goulash.)

ALSO FROM NEWCON PRESS

Blackthorn Winter – Liz Williams

Something is coming for the Fallow sisters, for their friends and their lovers, but they have no idea what, and their mother Alys is no help as she's gone wandering again, though she did promise to return by Christmas, and December is already here... In this sequel to *Comet Weather*, four fey sisters are drawn ever further from the familiar world of contemporary London and their Somerset home into darker realms where no one is who they seem and nothing is to be trusted...

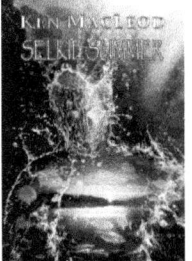

Selkie Summer – Ken MacLeod

Set on the Isle of Skye, Ken MacLeod's *Selkie Summer* is a rich contemporary fantasy steeped in Celtic lore, nuclear submarines and secrets. Seeking to escape Glasgow, student Siobhan Ross takes a holiday job on Skye, only to find herself the focus of unwanted attention, unwittingly embroiled in political intrigue and the shifting landscape of international alliances. At its heart, *Selkie Summer* is a love story: passionate, unconventional, and totally enchanting.

Frequencies of Existence – Andrew Hook

Andrew Hook sees the world through a different lens. He takes often mundane things and coaxes the reader to find strangeness and beauty in their form; he colours the world in surreal shades and leads the reader down discomforting paths where nothing is quite as it should be. *Frequencies of Existence* features twenty-four of his finest stories, including four that are original to this collection.

Ivory's Story – Eugen Bacon

A killer stalks the streets of Sydney, slaughtering innocents. The victims seem unconnected, yet Investigating Officer Ivory Tembo is convinced the killings are far from random. The case soon leads Ivory into places she never imagined. In order to stop the killings and save the life of the man she loves, she must reach deep into her past, uncover secrets of her heritage, break a demon's curse, and somehow unify two worlds.

ALSO BY IAN WATSON

Waters of Destiny – Ian Watson & Andy West

In this stunning novel, award winning author Ian Watson teams up with scientist and author Andy West to deliver a breathless blend of conspiracy theory, techno-thriller, historical fiction and the Da Vinci Code, telling an all too convincing tale of deceit, murder, and cataclysmic events that reach from the distant past to threaten all of our tomorrows, via a present day in which pandemic is used as a weapon...

The 1000 Year Reich – Ian Watson

Ian Watson, author of the very first novels in the Warhammer 40K universe, makes a welcome return to military SF with "In Golden Armour", one of three originals in this fabulous collection from the man who wrote the screen story to *AI: Artificial Intelligence* for Stanley Kubrick (filmed by Steven Spielberg). Expect the unexpected in these eghteen stories showcasing this multiple award-winning author at his best.

THE BELOVED
OF MY BELOVED

Ian Watson & Roberto Quaglia
Roberto Quaglia & Ian Watson

Beloved Of My Beloved – Ian Watson & Roberto Quaglia

A British SF author and an Italian surrealist collaborate to produce this most unlikely of books. Tattooed on a woman-sized tumour, these tales, told to it as bedtime stories, are by turns surreal, satiric, erotic, obscene, ingenious, hilarious, and quite, quite brilliant. Together, they combine to create a weird and wonderful love story, unlike anything told before. One component story, "The Beloved Time of Their Lives", won the BSFA Award for best short fiction.

Orgasmachine – Ian Watson

The first English language edition of Ian's long lost novel, which became a cult hit in Japan. Forget Stepford Wives; this goes way beyond anything seen in Stepford. Women as chattels, as customised sexslaves; bodies freakishly modified to their owners' dictates, personalities preset to order: the world of the Orgasmachine. But Jade and Mari escape their masters and dream of revenge, of revolution, of freedom...

www.newconpress.co.uk

Lightning Source UK Ltd.
Milton Keynes UK
UKHW011948211220
375665UK00002B/68